Dear Parent:

Congratulations! Your child is taking the first steps on an exciting journey. The destination? Independent reading!

STEP INTO READING® will help your child get there. The program offers five steps to reading success. Each step includes fun stories and colorful art. There are also Step into Reading Sticker Books, Step into Reading Math Readers, Step into Reading Phonics Readers, Step into Reading Write-In Readers, and Step into Reading Phonics Boxed Sets—a complete literacy program with something to interest every child.

Learning to Read, Step by Step!

Ready to Read   Preschool–Kindergarten
• big type and easy words • rhyme and rhythm • picture clues
For children who know the alphabet and are eager to begin reading.

Reading with Help   Preschool–Grade 1
• basic vocabulary • short sentences • simple stories
For children who recognize familiar words and sound out new words with help.

Reading on Your Own   Grades 1–3
• engaging characters • easy-to-follow plots • popular topics
For children who are ready to read on their own.

Reading Paragraphs   Grades 2–3
• challenging vocabulary • short paragraphs • exciting stories
For newly independent readers who read simple sentences with confidence.

Ready for Chapters   Grades 2–4
• chapters • longer paragraphs • full-color art
For children who want to take the plunge into chapter books but still like colorful pictures.

STEP INTO READING® is designed to give every child a successful reading experience. The grade levels are only guides. Children can progress through the steps at their own speed, developing confidence in their reading, no matter what their grade.

Remember, a lifetime love of reading starts with a single step!

Step into Reading, Random House, and the Random House colophon are registered trademarks of Random House, Inc.

Visit us on the Web!
StepIntoReading.com
randomhouse.com/kids

Educators and librarians, for a variety of teaching tools, visit us at randomhouse.com/teachers

ISBN: 978-0-7364-2847-7 (trade) — ISBN: 978-0-7364-8094-9 (lib. bdg.)

Printed in the United States of America
10 9 8 7 6 5 4 3 2 1

STEP INTO READING®

STEP 3

The Perfect Pumpkin Hunt

By Gail Herman

Illustrated by Adrienne Brown,
Loren Vasquez, and Manuela Razzi

Random House 🏠 New York

It was fall in Pixie Hollow.

Prilla loved fall.

There were so many fun things

to do!

She watched a squirrel hunt

for nuts.

Then she chased

falling leaves.

She jumped

onto a big oak leaf.

She took a ride as it fell

to the ground.

Prilla flipped
into a big leaf pile.
"Whee!" she cried.
Just then,
Queen Clarion flew over.
The Fall Ball was that evening.
She needed Prilla's help.
Prilla loved the Fall Ball!
There would be music, dancing,
and tasty fall treats.

Queen Clarion and Prilla flew
to the Home Tree.
All around them,
fairies were getting ready
for the ball.
Party talents hung streamers
made from grapevines.
Music talents tuned
reed whistles
and walnut drums.

In the kitchen,

Dulcie and the baking talents

put apple pies

on the windowsill

to cool.

Every fairy had a job to do.

Prilla was excited to hear

what her job would be.

Prilla and the queen landed
in the courtyard.

"Can you find the biggest, best,
most wonderful pumpkin
for the ball?"

Queen Clarion asked Prilla.

Prilla jumped for joy.

She had the best job of all!

The Fall Ball would begin

at sunset.

"There's not much time,"

the queen told Prilla.

"I'll hurry,"
said Prilla.
Then she flew off.
She was determined
to find the perfect pumpkin.

Just past the Home Tree,

Lily was clearing her garden.

Prilla waved hello.

"I have to find

the perfect pumpkin

for the Fall Ball,"

she said.

Lily was trying
to lift a big orange leaf.
She couldn't lift it alone.

Prilla stopped to help.

Together Prilla and Lily

moved the leaf

out of the garden.

Then they moved another,

and another.

"Now I have to fly!"

said Prilla.

She soared into the air.

"Thank you for your help!"

Lily called.

She waved goodbye.

Prilla flew
toward the pumpkin patch.
The sun was low in the sky.
She flapped her wings harder.
Just then,
she saw Beck sorting nuts
with a squirrel.

"This is for now,"
Beck said.
She placed a hazelnut
in a yellow basket.
"This is for winter."
Beck put a walnut
in a green basket.

There were so many nuts
to sort!
Beck would never finish
before the ball.
Prilla decided to help.

Prilla landed near Beck
and her squirrel friend.
Together the fairies sorted
every last nut.
Beck thanked Prilla
when they were done.
"It would have taken so long
without you!"

Prilla looked at the sky.

The sun was even lower now!

She had to find

the perfect pumpkin—and fast!

Prilla flew quickly

toward the pumpkin patch.

In the meadow,

she saw Tinker Bell and Pluck.

They were working on a big wagon.

Tink fixed an acorn-cap wheel.

Pluck filled the wagon with hay.

"This will be great for hayrides!"

Pluck called to Prilla.

Prilla agreed.

But it was hard work

for just two fairies.

Prilla stopped.

She held the wheel in place
for Tink.

She helped Pluck carry hay.

Finally,
the wagon was finished.
Prilla looked at the sky.
It was almost sunset!
She still had to find
the perfect pumpkin
for the ball!
Prilla took off again.

She flew as fast
as she could.
Finally,
she arrived
at the pumpkin patch.
She gasped.
There were pumpkins
as far as she could see.
The perfect one
had to be there!

Prilla flew from pumpkin
to pumpkin.

One pumpkin was too green.

One was too small.

One was too bumpy.

And one was too smelly.

Not one pumpkin was right.

Prilla was running out of time!

Suddenly,

Prilla spotted a pumpkin

at the edge of the patch.

It was big and round.

It was bright orange

and as smooth as glass.

Its stem was curved

in a pretty C shape.

"It's perfect!"

said Prilla.

She couldn't wait

to take it to the ball!

Prilla pushed.

She pulled.

She tugged.

The pumpkin didn't budge.

Prilla had an idea.
She took out her fairy dust
and sprinkled some
on the pumpkin.
The pumpkin slowly floated
off the ground.
Then it fell
with a thud.
The pumpkin was too big.

Prilla looked up one more time.

Pink and orange streaks

lit the sky.

"Sunset!" she cried.

She would never get the pumpkin

to the ball in time.

Suddenly, Prilla heard voices.

"We'll help!" they called.

It was Tink and Lily and Pluck.

Beck and her squirrel friend

were there, too.

Prilla had helped her friends.
Now they had come
to help her.
Together the fairies
rolled the pumpkin
onto the wagon.

42

"Ready!" called Pluck.

The squirrel pulled the wagon.

The fairies pushed.

The pumpkin was moving!

Prilla hoped they weren't

too late.

44

Just as the sun was setting,
the wagon rolled
into the courtyard.
Prilla gasped.
The courtyard looked beautiful!
Fireflies twinkled.
Red, orange, and yellow leaves
covered the ground.
Dried corncobs and gourds hung
from floating balloon carriers.

Prilla stopped the wagon.
She and her friends
rolled the pumpkin
onto the ground.
They lifted it
onto a pedestal.
Queen Clarion flew over.
"That really *is* the biggest,
best, most wonderful
pumpkin," she said.
"Let the Fall Ball begin!"

Prilla hugged her friends.
She had found
a wonderful pumpkin.
But her friends were
the most wonderful thing
of all.